This book belongs to ...

OXFORD
UNIVERSITY PRESS

Great Clarendon Street, Oxford, OX2 6DP,
United Kingdom

Oxford University Press is a department of the University of Oxford.
It furthers the University's objective of excellence in research, scholarship,
and education by publishing worldwide. Oxford is a registered trade mark of
Oxford University Press in the UK and in certain other countries

ISBN: 978-0-19-831026-6

1 3 5 7 9 10 8 6 4 2

Paper used in the production of this book is a natural, recyclable product made
from wood grown in sustainable forests. The manufacturing process conforms
to the environmental regulations of the country of origin.

Acknowledgements;
Series Editors: Kate Ruttle, Annemarie Young

READ WITH
**Biff,
Chip &
Kipper**

Rain Again
and Other Stories

Rain Again 6

The Rook and the Ring 28

The Real Floppy 50

The Old Tree Stump 72

OXFORD
UNIVERSITY PRESS

Tips for Reading Together

Children learn best when reading is fun.

- Talk about the title and the picture on the front cover.

- Identify the letter pattern *ai* in the title and talk about the sound it makes when you read it.

- Look at the *ai* words on page 8. Say the sounds in each word and then say the word (e.g. *r-ai-n, rain*).

- Read the story and find the words with the letters *ai* in them.

- Do the fun activity at the end of the story.

Children enjoy re-reading stories and this helps to build their confidence.

Have fun!

After you have read the story, find the ten birds in the pictures.

The main sound practised in this book is 'ai' as in *rain, pail* and *wait*.

For more hints and tips on helping your child become a successful and enthusiastic reader look at our website www.oxfordowl.co.uk.

Rain Again

Written by Roderick Hunt
Illustrated by Nick Schon,
based on the original characters
created by Roderick Hunt and Alex Brychta

OXFORD
UNIVERSITY PRESS

Read these words

again   pail

pain   rain

nail   wait

tail

Rain again, rain again.

Get in my den.

Rain on the roof.

Rain in my den.

Get a pail.

Rain again, rain again.

Rain in my shed.

Fix the roof.

Get a nail.

Rain again, rain again.

So much rain.

Rain in my boots.

I am wet, wet, wet.

Rain in my hair.

But I am not wet.

Floppy is wet.

No, Floppy!

Talk about the story

Odd one out

Which two of these things doesn't have
the 'ai' sound in the middle of the word?

(Answer to odd one out: ball, fish)

Tips for Reading Together

Children learn best when reading is fun.

- Talk about the title and the picture on the front cover.
- Identify the letter pattern *oo* in the title and talk about the sound it makes when you read it.
- Look at the *oo* and *ie* words on page 30. Say the sounds in each word and then say the word (e.g. *t-oo-k, took*).
- Read the story and find the words with the letters *oo* and *ie* in them.
- Do the fun activity at the end of the story.

Children enjoy re-reading stories and this helps to build their confidence.

Have fun!

After you have read the story, find the five ladybirds in the pictures.

The main sounds practised in this book are 'oo' as in *rook* and 'ie' as in *tie*.

For more hints and tips on helping your child become a successful and enthusiastic reader look at our website www.oxfordowl.co.uk.

The Rook
and the Ring

Written by Roderick Hunt
Illustrated by Nick Schon,
based on the original characters
created by Roderick Hunt and Alex Brychta

OXFORD
UNIVERSITY PRESS

Read these words

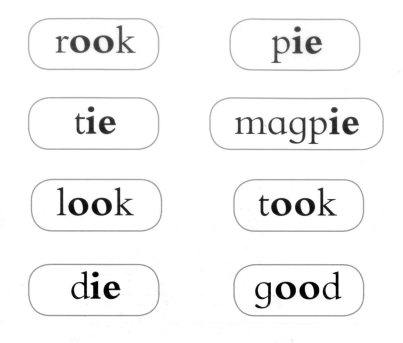

r**oo**k	p**ie**
t**ie**	magp**ie**
look	t**oo**k
d**ie**	g**oo**d

A rook sat on a pot.

It had a bad wing.

Chip got Mum and Dad.

Mum took the rook.

The Rook
and the Ring

Written by Roderick Hunt
Illustrated by Nick Schon,
based on the original characters
created by Roderick Hunt and Alex Brychta

OXFORD

UNIVERSITY PRESS

Read these words

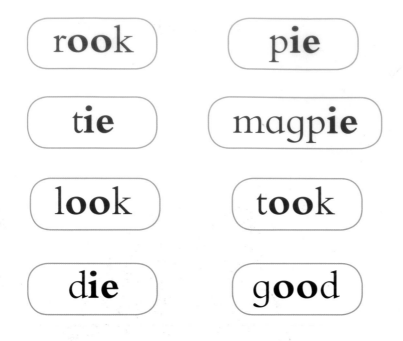

rook

pie

tie

magpie

look

took

die

good

A rook sat on a pot.

It had a bad wing.

Chip got Mum and Dad.

Mum took the rook.

"Let's call him Ron," said Biff.

Biff and Chip fed Ron the rook.

Dad let the rook go.

Mum was cooking.

Mum took off her ring.

A magpie took the ring.

Mum ran out.

Mum and Dad ran.

Biff, Chip and Floppy ran.

The magpie went to a wood.

Ron the rook got the ring.

The magpie shot off.

"Well, well. I got my ring,"
said Mum.

Talk about the story

What was wrong with the rook?

How did Mum lose her ring?

How did Mum get her ring back?

What things have you lost and then found again?

Spot the difference

Find the five differences in the pictures of Ron the rook and the nest.

(Answer to spot the difference: tail, paper clip, eye, beak, colour of bottle top)

Tips for Reading Together

Children learn best when reading is fun.

- Talk about the title and the picture on the front cover.
- Look through the pictures together and discuss what you think the story might be about.
- Read the story together, pointing to the words and inviting your child to join in.
- Give lots of praise as your child reads with you, and help them when necessary.
- Try different ways of helping if they get stuck on a word. For example: refer to the picture, or read the first sound or syllable of the word, or read the whole sentence and focus on the meaning.
- Do the fun activity at the end of the story.

Children enjoy re-reading stories and this helps to build their confidence.

Have fun!

After you have read the story, find the ten seashells in the pictures.

This book includes these useful common words:

children his let's made said

For more hints and tips on helping your child become a successful and enthusiastic reader look at our website www.oxfordowl.co.uk.

The Real Floppy

Written by Roderick Hunt
Illustrated by Alex Brychta

OXFORD
UNIVERSITY PRESS

The children ran onto the sand.

"Let's play here," said Biff.

Wilma threw a ball and
Floppy ran after it.

Floppy ran back with the ball.

Dad ran up. "Stop!" he said.

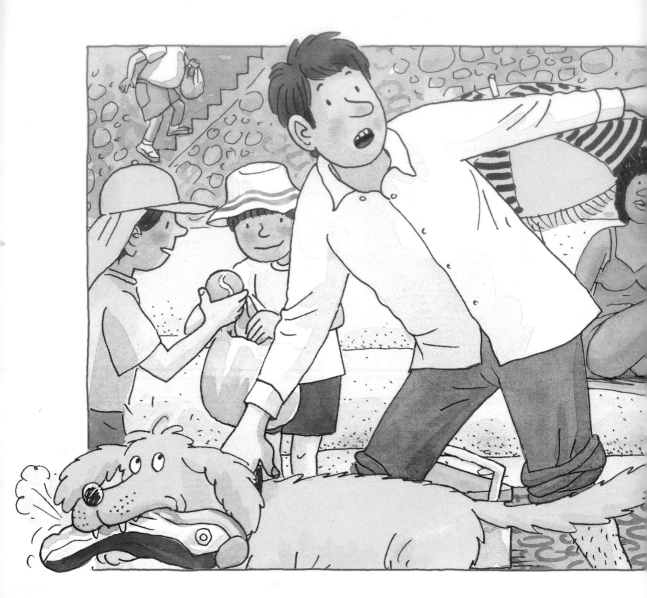

"Look at that," said Dad.

"Dogs can't go on the sand."

"Poor Floppy!" said Mum.
"I'll take him for a walk."

The children were upset.

They didn't want Floppy to go.

"Let's give Mum a surprise,"
said Dad.

They made a big pile of sand.
Everyone helped.

"Now let's pat it flat," said Dad.

"Let's make his head," said Biff.

"And his ears," said Chip.

"Let's put in his eyes," said Wilf.

"And make his tail," said Kipper.

Mum came back.

"Surprise! Surprise!" said Biff.

"A Floppy made of sand!"
said Mum.

"It's a good sand dog,"
said Kipper.
"But I love the real Floppy best."

Talk about the story

Why wasn't Floppy allowed on the beach?

What was Mum's surprise? Why was it a good surprise?

Why were the children happy when they were making Mum's surprise?

What have you made out of sand? Were you proud of it?

Picture puzzle

How many things can you find beginning with the same sound as the 's' in sea?

(Answer to picture puzzle: sail, sand, sandcastle, sea, sunglasses)

Tips for Reading Together

Children learn best when reading is fun.

- Talk about the title and the picture on the front cover.

- Look through the pictures together and discuss what you think the story might be about.

- Read the story together, pointing to the words and inviting your child to join in.

- Give lots of praise as your child reads with you, and help them when necessary.

- Try different ways of helping if they get stuck on a word. For example: refer to the picture, or read the first sound or syllable of the word, or read the whole sentence and focus on the meaning.

- Do the fun activity at the end of the story.

Children enjoy re-reading stories and this helps to build their confidence.

Have fun!

After you have read the story, find these ten minibeasts in the pictures.

This book includes these useful common words:

come didn't pull want

For more hints and tips on helping your child become a successful and enthusiastic reader look at our website www.oxfordowl.co.uk.

The Old Tree Stump

Written by Roderick Hunt
Illustrated by Alex Brychta

OXFORD
UNIVERSITY PRESS

"That old stump has to go,"
said Dad. Benn

Dad pulled the old stump,
but it didn't come up.

Dad called Mum to help.
"I'll push it. You pull it,"
said Dad.

"When I say pull," said Dad,
"I want you to pull!"

Mum pulled and pulled, but
the stump didn't come up.

Dad called Biff.

"I want you to pull," said Dad.

Mum and Biff pulled…
but the stump *still* didn't come up.

Dad wanted Chip to help.

"When I shout pull," said Dad,

"I want you to pull."

They all pulled…

but the stump *still* didn't come up.

Kipper wanted to help.

"Come on, then," said Dad.

"When I shout pull… PULL!"

They pulled and they pulled…
but the stump *still* didn't come up.

"I'll pull as well," said Dad.
"When I yell pull... PULL!"

They all pulled and pulled…
but the stump *still* didn't come up.

Floppy saw a bone.

He dug and he dug, and…

up came the stump!

BUMP!

"Good old Floppy!" said Chip.

Talk about the story

How did the stump come up in the end?

Which part of the story did you find the funniest?

Have you ever read the Enormous Turnip? How is it like this story?

What jobs do you help with at home?

Picture puzzle

Which things don't rhyme with snail?

(Answer to picture puzzle: snake, spade)

Read with Biff, Chip and Kipper
The UK's best-selling home reading series

Phonics

First Stories

	Phonics	First Stories
Level 1 Getting ready to read	Kipper's Alphabet I Spy · Chip's Letter Sounds · Biff's Wonder Words · Floppy's Fun Phonics	Get On · Floppy Did This! · Up You Go · Six in a Bed
Level 2 Starting to read	I am Kipper · Cat in a Bag · The Red Hen · The Fizz-Buzz	Funny Fish · Silly Races! · The Snowman · Dad's Birthday
Level 3 Becoming a reader	Such a Fuss · Shops · The Sing Song · The Backpack	Poor Old Rabbit · I Can Trick a Tiger · Super Dad · Floppy and the Bone
Level 4 Developing as a reader	Wet Feet · The Moon Jet · The Red Coat · Quick! Quick!	Missing! · The Raft Race · Dragon Danger · The Spaceship
Level 5 Building confidence in reading	Egg Fried Moon · Craig · Seawink · Dolphin Rescue	Hungry Floppy · Husky Adventure · Trapped! · Looking after Gran
Level 6 Reading with confidence	Gran's New Blue Shoes · Ice City · Save Pudding Wood · Uncle Max	Hairy-Scary Monster · Mountain Rescue · The Lost Voice · Secret of the Sands

Phonics stories help children practise their sounds and letters, as they learn to do in school.

First Stories have been specially written to provide practice in reading everyday language.

Read with Biff, Chip and Kipper Collections:

Up You Go and other Stories · Six in a Bed and other Stories · Funny Fish and other Stories · The Fizz-Buzz and other Stories

Floppy and the Bone and other Stories · I Can Trick a Tiger and other Stories · The Moon Jet and other Stories · Dragon Danger and other Stories

2 Phonics and 2 First Stories in every collection

Phonics support

Flashcards are a really fun way to practise phonics and build reading skills. **Age 3+**

My Phonics Kit is designed to support you and your child as you practise phonics together at home. It includes stickers, workbooks, interactive eBooks, support for parents and more! **Age 5+**

Read Write Inc. Phonics: A range of fun rhyming stories to support decoding skills. **Age 4+**

Songbirds Phonics: Lively and engaging phonics stories from Children's Laureate, Julia Donaldson. **Age 4+**

Help your child's reading with essential tips, advice on phonics and free eBooks
www.oxfordowl.co.uk